THIS BOOK BELONGS TO:

....

Dedicated to 'The Burper'er,' Tijsje,
who burps for good reason and good cause – Chris O'M

A publication of Red Rabbit Rises Publishing
Inverness, Scotland, United Kingdom

Printed and bound via IngramSpark

ISBN: 978-1-9161477-3-7

'The Burper'er' available in a range of formats.
For this and other titles, please visit www.redrabbitrises.com

RED RABBIT RISES
PUBLISHING

the BURPER'ER

BY CHRIS O'MALLEY

ILLUSTRATED BY PHOEBE ROZE

She was called "Little Baby Burper'er"
from the day that she was born
all tiny, shiny and new.
She could burp to a size
that didn't fit her body -
although it wasn't possible
it still was simply
just plain true.

Her belly would rumble
　　this deep gurgling sound,
　　like water running fast and loud
　　deep under the ground.
Her chest would blow up
　　like those big bubble-gum throat frogs
　　it would grow huge like a big
　　almost bursting balloon -
And when you thought she'd explode
　　she'd let out a burp

BUUUURRRRPPpP!!!

　　that would feel like it
　　was rattling your insides -
　　that would shake
　　all the furniture in the room!

BAAAARRRR!!!

As she got bigger
     the burps got louder.
Instead of being embarrassed
     she got prouder and prouder.
She found she could play with burping -
     she made it an art! She did it with poise!
Rumbling deep like a lion
     growling across the savanna
     out of all her burps
     was her very most favourite noise!

Then one day in school
	a bully picked on her friend in class,
	and immediately The Burper'er
	solved the problem fast!

The class all saw
	and then heard her belly rumble,
	then saw her lips wave,

wibble and wobble

	From there
	that bully didn't stand a chance -
	houses of cards
	were harder to topple!

She had helped and saved her friend,
	it was easy, short and painless,
	and in that moment of helping her friend,
	all over school she was famous!

And from that moment,
 she knew it -
 her doubt was simply zero.
She knew then that when
 she grew up,
 she'd be a Superhero!
With a big red "B" on her front,
 and a cape on her back.
But not with underpants on the outside -
 that was just silly!
 She wouldn't be having
 any of that!

She'd burp at the baddies,
    blowing them over,
    and straight into the back
    of the police van.

BBBBUUUURRRRRRPPPPPPP!!!

All of the people
    would be happier and safer,
    they'd all be
    great big "Burper'er" fans.

She saw it all clearly,
    she was "Born to burp."
    She now had a plan -
    she was not for turning!
But unfortunately just then
    her teacher came into class,
    and asked them to sit,
    and focus on their learning.

The Burper'er raised her hand,
    and she told her teacher
    that she'd already learned
    a big big thing!
    That she had just
    learned her fate!
But her teacher told her
    that Superhero work was
    disruptive in class,
    that being "The Burper'er"
    would just have to wait.

She thought her teacher
    wouldn't believe that she could fly
    even if right then and there
    she grew great big flapping wings.
But it really didn't matter,
    for she was now famous
    as "The Burper'er" –
    having to wait
    in class as a child
    was just one of those things.

She felt her stomach rumble,
  felt her lips **wibble**
  and then **wobble**
  felt her throat swell up with air,
  like a ship's sail in a sharp breeze.
She then laughed to herself
  as she realised
  she was one
  of those good superheroes.
Or at least that she was
  going to give
  being good
  a really good go.

From that day at school
    she knew how to burp -
    and she knew that knowing
    was one of the keys!
Then she let out a quiet long burp
    that felt like a warm gentle
    summer breeze.
She now knew how to control her burps,
    the Burper'er could do that now,
    she could burp with style.
    she could burp with ease.

She knew all this,
    but as their teacher stood,
    and taught the class,
    she knew that
    the rest of the world
    would have to wait
    a little longer to see
    the great things in the future
    that The Burper'er could now see.

BBB